W9-BSD-004

Grandma's in the Garbage

written by
Steve and Mica Westover

illustrated by
Mica Westover

Published by Missouri Star Quilt Company

Missouri Star Quilt Company
114 N Davis
Hamilton, Mo. 64644
888-571-1122
info@missouriquiltco.com
Published and Printed in the USA

Cenveo Publisher Services
2901 Byrdhill Road
Richmond, VA 23228

©Copyright Steve and Mica Westover, 2015
All Rights Reserved.

First published in the United States of America by Missouri Star Quilt Company 2015.
Grandma's in the Garbage / written by Steve and Mica Westover, illustrated by Mica Westover
Summary: Grandma creates a memory quilt for her granddaughter from scraps of
unforgettable fabrics.

Except in the United States of America, this book is sold subject to the condition that is shall
not, by way of trade or otherwise, be lent, re-sold, hired out, or otherwise circulated without
the publisher's prior consent in any form of binding or cover or other than that in which it is
published and without a similar condition including this condition being imposed on the
subsequent purchaser.

ISBN - 978-1-63224-011-8

For information regarding the CPSIA on this printed material call:
203-595-3636 and provide reference # LANC – 639242

For our remarkable children
who remind us every day why they are
our treasures.

—— *special thanks* ——

Natalie, Sarah, and Jenny

Thank you for your encouragement and
helping to make a dream come true.

Grandma, why are you digging that
dress out of the garbage? **YUCK!**

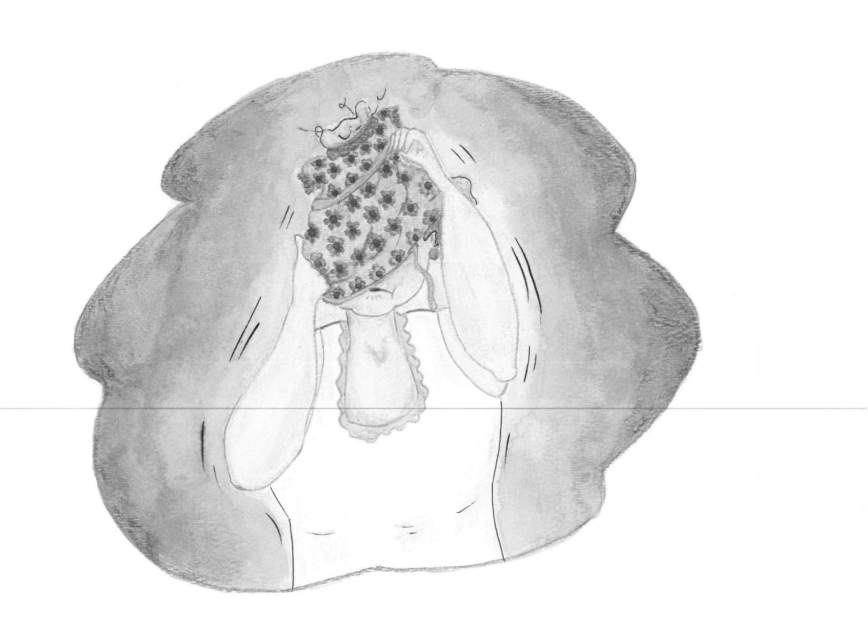

Strange. Why would there be treasure in the trash? That dress will **NEVER** fit her!

Hmmm. I wonder how long she has been doing this?

I wonder if she's going through other people's garbage?

Oh no! What would the neighbors think if they saw
Grandma snooping for treasure in their trash?

She could get in **HUGE** trouble!

I don't want Grandma to go to jail. I would be so sad if she went away for a long time.

was searching for she simply replied, "Trea-sures." Concerned about the woman's unusual behavior, Detective Scanlan booked her into the City hold-

Girl Pleads For Grandma's Releas

MSQC Teaches Students to Quilt

GER goes to... ger Dive

12 Year Old Win. County Quilting

L DISPLAYS N HISTORY

Governor Visits Hamilton

Late Saturday night, Hamilton City Police arrested an elderly woman digging through her neighbor's garbage. When asked what she was searching for she simply repl

Declares Hamilton, MO Quilt Town

13

I must save her from a life of crime!

"Grandma, **STOP EVERYTHING!**

We need to talk." "You will **NOT** find

treasure in our garbage and you will not

find it in our neighbors garbage either."

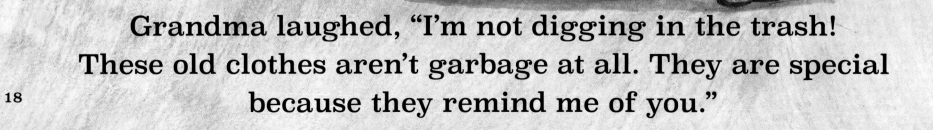
Grandma laughed, "I'm not digging in the trash! These old clothes aren't garbage at all. They are special because they remind me of you."

"This dress reminds me of you
as an itty, bitty baby. So precious."

"You took this blankie everywhere you went."

"You even took it
swimming."

"I remember this tie! Daddy wore it
when I was sick. He took care of me!"

"Your mother's apron
reminds me that your mom
will do anything to take
care of you."

"I remember when we
made monster cookies with
sprinkles on them!"

"Grandma, this is for you.
You can have my treasure."

Thank you, dear!
I have something for you too. . .

"I made this special memory quilt as a treasure just for you."

"Whoa...it's beautiful! Look...I see daddy's tie, and there's my blankie. That's mom's apron, and my baby dress! **I LOVE IT!**"

29

I love you, sweetie. You are my treasure
and I want you to always remember.

THE END